NEVER BE LONELY AGAIN

CARIETTA DORSCH

UNVEILING NIGHTMARES PRESS

"It just seemed so bizarre to me this obsession that I had been thinking about and wanting...all the parts are there and they make it possible to make it happen," - Jeff Dahmer

Contents

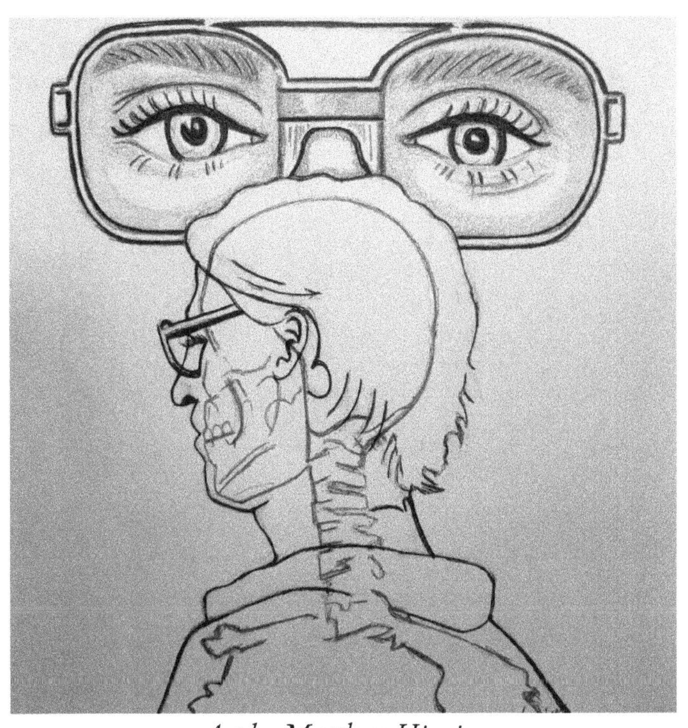

Art by Matthew Higgins

FOREWORD

Splatterpark by Asher Dark and Carietta Dorsch was my first introduction to Carietta's writing. Immediately, I was impressed by her ability to craft a multifaceted story with all the bells and whistles of a true expert in the Splatterpunk genre. Her tales all included a slew of eccentric characters festering in a hellish trailer park with all the gore, depravity, and fecal matter a reader as twisted as I could ever yearn for.

However, upon scrubbing my brain clean of the stomach churning debauchery, I saw a glimmer of a skillset that went deeper. While I love a good poop story as much as the next girl, what really hooked me on Carietta as an author was her prose. Her ability to show the reader a scene, a character, or a setting instead of *telling* them had me craving more.

As fate would have it, our professional relationship and personal friendship collided at the connection of none other than our common interest in the famed midwestern serial killer, Jeffrey Dahmer. From the time I started delving into the cruelties of mankind, I adopted a bizarre fascination with this particular boogeyman. There is a melancholic complexity to the chain of events that comprised Dahmer's life. One that both breaks my heart and reminds me to hug my loved ones a little closer.

From the late 1970's to the early 1990's, this notorious predator ended the lives of 17 young men long before their time. He often prowled the streets eager to capture an unsuspecting youth through manipulation and sexual encounters before proceeding with dismemberment and cannibalism. The spree of the Milwaukee Monster ceased when he was caught with an apartment full of Polaroids from his assaults, a 55 gallon drum containing acid and fragments of his victims, and several body parts preserved in his freezer.

I consider myself a seasoned Splatterpunk reader and one, at that, not easily offended. Through my journey navigating and exploring this genre, I have read some of the most vile fiction in existence. However, one thing I have learned along the way is that there is often a sprinkling of true real life horror laced within the pages of these novellas. Whether it be underlying themes of mental illness, abuse, or other traumas, it is pertinent to respect the craft of a writer who can convey these messages with grace while still implementing their abilities to entertain.

What I challenge my fellow readers to understand is that this is not a one note work. When I first read *Never Be Lonely Again*, I felt a range of emotions centered around the unbearable ache of loneliness that came to me as an unexpected sucker punch. Aside from that, I adventured into topics of conformity, mental illness, rejection, sexuality, and acceptance of one's true self.

While our main character's actions, much of which mirror Dahmer's, are unfathomable to me, I cannot deny the interest of traveling into the psyche of someone who was abandoned and left to face the depth of their darkness. I simultaneously managed to feel the neglect from her parents through their abandonment and lack of acknowledgment, the untreated illness lurking in her brain, and the eventual embracing of one's isolation. More so, as starkly different as it was, I felt this with similar intensity to the grief as I mourned her victims.

Dorsch's ability to confront such heavy topics through the grace of her writing pushes her readers to peel back the layers of humanity. She created this Dahmer inspired work with an elegant finesse that leaves a lasting impact. Most importantly, she took the concept of a famed serial killer's life, implemented her own originality, and did so without glorifying a man who destroyed the lives of many individuals and their families.

Without further ado, I invite you to entertain the complexity of life and the impact of your own truths through this piece. Savor it, explore it, and then sit with it a while. For all of its intensity and brutality, there is an unconventional beauty in Carietta's words.

By Sarah DeRosa

Never Be Lonely Again

As I pull the drill bit out of her skull, I hear a wet popping sound and watch a dribble of blood ooze out of the hole I just made. Bits of brain clings to the spiraled metal, and I close my fist around a clump of hair. I squeeze the moist glob and feel the liquid seep between my fingers.

Dark thoughts consume my mind: The desire to possess, control, consume. It's a hunger that can never be satisfied, a thirst that can never be quenched.

But it can be temporarily sated.

Looking down at her body, I know my cravings will be silenced, at least for tonight.

I lift my teapot off the coffee table and pour water into the hole. Determination drives my desire to make my own zombie, one that will love me and be with me forever.

The water flows out of the hole and down her face. After washing the wound, I'm able to see what I'm doing. I put the teapot down and grab the drill again.

A squishing, sucking sound escapes the hole as I slide the drill bit inside, and a red-tinted seepage flows out around the metal. When I feel a soft resistance I know I have reached her brain.

I add steady pressure to the trigger until the drill tears apart the gray mass within her skull to eat away the bone. When I yank the drill out of her head, a spray of blood splatters my face.

I push my finger in and out of the hole as if I'm making love to her. My panties stick to my pussy as I grow wet.

Leaning down, I push my mouth closer, taking all of her in: her scent, her taste. Flicking my tongue across her skull's opening, I push her panties down. Putting my lips around the wound, I twirl my tongue inside the jagged hole. I congratulate myself for buying that spade bit.

Pleasure is like passionate love, subjective, private, and not the same for any two people. Like sidewalks, many on the same one, few taking the same route, only passing and never seeing each other again.

My breath hitches as I run my tongue up and down the leaking gap, tasting the warm coppery tang only makes me moister. I slide my tongue inside as I pull my finger out. I hold her head in place, using the thumb from my other hand to massage her clit, as my tongue moves in and out of the oozing opening. My breathing becomes quick, labored pants, then seems to stop until I release a deep moan and come.

I continue to lick and tease, feeling my pussy clench and contort with orgasm, as my panties flood with my juices.

Sliding my finger inside her head, pulling it out, I shove it inside my pussy. It's as if I can feel her thoughts swirling inside me, making me shiver with delight.

My sex is wet, my clit is firm, and my lips are swollen, opening like a flower as I push my finger deeper, painting its moist petals with her memories and creating our own.

I pick up my circular saw. The room is filled with the sound of tearing flesh, a sound I cherish. Her body flops around, jerking with the vibration of the saw.

A geyser of crimson erupts from her throat, painting the front of me. The metallic scent of blood fills the air, overpowering my senses. I watch in fascination as the crimson liquid cascades down her lifeless body, pooling on the couch beneath her.

Licking my lips, and tasting what was splattered on me is invigorating. Feeling the blood trickle down my chin makes my pussy clench with the need for more, and a moan escapes my lips.

I can't tear my eyes away from the magnificent sight before me. The saw continues, tearing through flesh and bone with relentless speed. Each movement sends trembles of ecstasy down my spine as if the blade itself is whispering sweet nothings in my ear.

Her head drops to the floor with a thud, and I let go of the trigger. Placing the saw on the coffee table, I pull my shirt off. Unhooking my bra, I toss it aside and lay on top of her, naked and aflame.

I kiss her open neck tentatively, yet eagerly.

I lick the jagged bone that protrudes.

I kiss my way down her body and suck on her nipple.

I explore her with my hands.

I stick my left hand inside her neck and push down into the mass of destroyed meat the saw created. Her body resists, connective tissues struggling to hold muscle and tissue together, but blood lubricates my arm and I can slide it into the tight space.

The muscle pressing against my arm reminds me of my pussy tightening as I approach climax. It seems to beg me to explore deeper. A world of new textures opens to me: stringy muscle, silky fascia, rubbery arteries.

Time stands still as I explore her, our bodies becoming one in a whirlwind of bliss.

My other hand reaches for my pussy as I lick the blood overflowing from her wound. As my moans grow louder, I push a third finger inside, cupping my sex, and imagining her doing this to me. I push deeper into myself as I push deeper into her.

I come, the sensation bursting from deep within me, escaping every pore as I collapse onto the couch next to her, sweating, leaking, and wanting more.

· · · • • • • · ·

Finding myself, once again unable to concentrate on my freshman project, I opened my last beer and listened to my parents as if they were a radio teleplay.

"What the fuck are you doing, Joyce?" my dad's voice echoed from the kitchen.

"I seen them, and I'm going to follow them!" my mom's shrill voice drilled through my ears as if she were in the room with me.

"Follow who?"

"The FBI, Lionel. They were out there, and I'm going to face them."

"There's no fucking FBI outside." I could picture my dad pushing his glasses up his nose as he always did when angry. "Goddamn it, Joyce, we can't be doing this every week in front of her!"

"Of who?"

"Your daughter, Joyce, your daughter. Unless you forgot." His voice nearly broke.

"I haven't forgotten. That was the worst nine months of my life!" Her words cut deeper than any knife. I knew her pregnancy had been difficult, but to hear I was the worst part of her life was saddening.

I couldn't take it anymore. I needed to escape, to find some peace and quiet away from their constant bickering.

Slipping out the back door, I made my way into the woods behind our house. The trees provided a comforting canopy, shielding me from the harsh reality of my parents' arguments. I found my way to the little shed I had built years ago, a sanctuary where I kept my taxidermy supplies.

As I entered the shed, the familiar smell of musty fur and dried blood enveloped me. I ran my fingers over the bones of the animals I had collected and preserved, finding solace in their silent presence. But as I continued to touch the bones, I felt a stirring deep inside me. This wasn't the first time, but the sensation was still new, still foreign.

I turned the small radio on and was welcomed by The Everly Brothers 'All I Have to Do is Dream'. I felt a primal urge that I couldn't ignore. I began to play with the bones, rubbing my fingers across them, memorizing their texture. And as I did, I felt an unfamiliar arousal building inside me.

I couldn't resist the temptation. Touching myself with the bones, feeling their cold, hard surfaces against my skin made me shiver with pleasure. The sensation was a mix of pleasure and taboo that sent ripples down my spine.

I lost myself in the moment, consumed by a desire I couldn't explain. The bones became my partners in a forbidden dance, their shapes and textures driving me to new heights of ecstasy. I unbuttoned my pants and pulled my panties down. I laid down on the floor, hesitated at first, unsure of what I was about to do. But as I lay back on the wood floor, the bone in my hand, I couldn't resist the urge any longer. Slowly, I began to use it like a dildo, each stroke offering a new girth, a new length, and a new level of pleasure as the tapered bone slid in and out of me.

I closed my eyes and let myself be consumed by the sensations. The bone slid in and out of me effortlessly, filling me in ways I had never experienced before. I moaned softly, my body arching with each thrust, my mind clouded with desire.

I lost track of time as I pleasured myself with the bone, each movement sending waves of ecstasy through me. I let go of all inhibitions and allow myself to fully embrace the pleasure. I moved the bone faster and faster, feeling the tension building inside me until finally, I reached a peak of ecstasy that I had never known before.

As I reached the peak of my pleasure, I let out a cry of release, my body trembling with the intensity of my orgasm.

I lay there, spent and satisfied, the bone still in my hand, a smile playing on my lips.

Suddenly, another orgasm hit me as the tip of the bone slid across my clit when I pulled it out. I knew I had found a new kind of release in the darkness of my life. I felt a sense of empowerment wash over me, knowing that I had discovered a new way to pleasure myself. I put the tip of the bone to my lips and sucked my juices from it as if I were sucking the marrow out of the bone itself.

A release that was all my own, away from the chaos of my parents fighting and the constraints of society's expectations of me and what the world deemed normal. This was mine, *I thought as I licked my lips*

I emerged from the shed, making my way back to the house. I knew I had found a secret world of pleasure that was mine and mine alone. And in that moment, I felt a sense of freedom I had never known before.

And then, I wondered, what would it be like with a person?

· · • • · • • · ·

Bang!
What.
Bang!
The.

Bang!

Fuck!

Is that the air-conditioner again?

Bang! Bang!

My eyes fly open and I look around. The knocking grows louder with each passing second, making my head hurt worse than the hangover. The body is still lying next to me, flies starting to hover around her open neck. I look down to see my own body covered in dried blood, and our legs are intertwined like any other couple's.

Shit! I am not ready for visitors.

"Who is it?" I yell from the couch as panic courses through my veins.

"The landlord!"

"One second!"

Fuck, fuck, fuck, fuck, fuck!

I get up from the couch and throw a blanket over the carnage before approaching the door. Grabbing another blanket, I wrap it around myself to hide the blood-soaked clothes.

Is there blood on my face? Of course, there is.

Bang! Bang! Bang! Bang!

"Hold on!"

A can of disinfecting wipes is by the door. I know the chemicals will hurt my skin, but I don't see a choice.

Bracing myself, I wipe my face, the wet liquid oozing off the wipe and running down my neck. The third wipe comes up clean, and I finally reach for the door.

I slowly open it, making sure the chains are in place to prevent him from seeing more than he has to.

I'm greeted by my overweight landlord standing there with a look of annoyance that hits me at eye level.

"Hey, Colin, how are you?" I ask with a smile.

"Do you know why I'm up here?" he asks as he scratches his balding head, and emphasizes the word 'why'.

"No, but I'm always glad to see you..."

"Cut the crap," he nearly yells, his face growing redder by the second. "Your neighbors say your apartment smells like something died..."

"Oh, that, sorry. I had some meat go bad on me, and I haven't made it to the dumpster yet." I avoid meeting his eyes.

He huffs, much like a disbelieving parent, before saying, "Last month a fish died, now it's bad meat." He waves his hands in frustration. "Just get it clean."

"I will. Sorry."

As Colin stomps away, I shut the door and make sure all five locks are secure, then begin to clean up the evidence.

Walking back to the body on the couch, I pick up the meat cleaver next to the stovetop. Placing her head on the coffee table, I let her watch me as I cut and chop into her body.

As I trace the blade along her skin, a crimson creek flows from each cut I make. The sight of her blood spilling out only fuels my desire, igniting a primal urge within me. The metallic scent of blood fills the air, mingling with the musky aroma of my own sweat and her decomposition.

I watch as the red liquid pools on her skin, puddling in her navel, and in the crevice of her throat. Each cut I make only serves to heighten the intensity of our connection, binding us together in a twisted dance of pleasure and delusion.

Her blood glistening in the dim light only fuels my need. I know what I am doing is wrong, but the hunger inside me is too strong to resist.

As I cut out pieces of meat from her body, the flesh peels away from the wound with surprising ease. The thought of consuming her flesh sends quivers down the length of my tongue and makes my taste buds sing in approval. Placing these pieces aside, I chop her into small pieces to make it easier for the acid.

I have a blue barrel filled with homemade acid in my bedroom to dissolve meat, bones, and anything else I need to. The stench of decay and chemicals hangs in the air when I open the lid, the sweet smell of companionship once known.

I begin plopping pieces of her into the barrel, careful not to splash. The ripples it makes remind me of the rumpled blanket on the couch.

Watching the meat disintegrate, I let out a low, guttural moan, relishing in the passion we had before the dismembering. Licking my lips, I watch the flesh melt away, leaving nothing but a sludgy, unrecognizable mess. This sludge I can keep forever. It will never leave, and will always be by my side.

The last piece is her head. It bobs and floats in the bubbles of the dissolving skin and bone as if she is taking one last bubble bath. Her head turns in the death water until her eyes stare out toward me. She looks sad as if she really wants to stay.

"You will," I whisper aloud. I want to reassure her that I'll never leave her.

My stomach begins growling, and I know I need to eat. I close the lid and lock it in place.

Walking into the kitchen, I see the chunk of thigh meat I'd left in the skillet. With two eggs and some hot sauce, I begin to make breakfast.

You'd think human meat would cook differently than cow or pig, but you'd be wrong. If you can cook an animal, you can cook a person.

The aroma of sizzling steak fills the air, making my stomach rumble in anticipation. I watch the meat searing in the skillet's heat, the rendered fat popping and hissing in the hot pan reminding me of popcorn. My mouth waters as the sizzle becomes something hypnotic. The sound arouses my senses, heightening my excitement for the meal to come.

I sit staring at the empty chair across from me. The silence is deafening, and the loneliness weighs on my heart. Standing, I place a second set of utensils and a napkin on the empty spot, pretending that someone will join me for dinner.

I know I am alone, but I can't help but imagine how it would feel to have someone sitting across from me, sharing a meal and conversation. The thought brings a bittersweet ache to my chest, a longing for companionship that seems out of reach. I add some hot sauce to a forkful of meat before sliding the fork into my mouth. In that first bite, the flavors explode in my mouth, bringing back memories of the night before.

As I savor each mouthful, I am grateful for the process of cooking and the joy it brings me. The steak on my plate is not just a meal but a labor of love, a reminder of the simple pleasures that can be found.

The taste of life runs across my taste buds.

Her childhood drips down my throat.

Her dreams, her goals, they all swirl around inside me.

She is a permanent part of me.

I finish my meal and clear the table, leaving the second set of utensils untouched. I can't bring myself to put them away as if by leaving them out, I can hold onto the fleeting illusion of company for just a little longer.

Retreating to the living room, I sink into the couch and stare at the blank television. Silence fills the room and does little to dispel the emptiness surrounding me. I long for someone to share this moment with, to laugh and talk, and simply be present.

I could turn on the television and drown myself in nonsense, but I don't have to work until tomorrow, and I decide to enjoy a few drinks at the club.

Walking the sidewalks, I can't help but notice everyone seems so happy. Talking on phones or chatting with their partners, they all wear smiles. I can't remember the last time I felt truly happy. The only thing that comes to mind is when my parents divorced. They both left that same week, seeming to forget about me in the empty house. I was alone but in a good way.

For the first time, I was free.

....

I was on a joyride when I saw her.

I always had the fantasy of finding a hitchhiker, but today it seemed my fantasy was becoming reality. Tipping the can skyward, I finished my beer and threw the can out of the window before pulling up next to her.

"Where you going?" I asked over the music.

"You going west?"

"Sure." I couldn't believe it. It was really happening. *"Hop in."*

"I'm Stephanie," she said. She opened the door, hesitating a moment before saying, "You aren't one of those Manson girls, are ya?"

"No," I laughed. *"I'm just a Wisconsin woman. Come on, we'll stop for drinks at my place if you want."*

"Oh, fuck yeah," she giggled. "Sorry." She sat down and closed the door.

"It's okay. I've heard the word 'fuck' before," I said with a smirk.

Driving down the road, I kept catching her glancing at me until finally, she sighed. "Can I ask you something?"

"Sure," I said, lighting a cigarette. "Smoke?"

"*Yeah,*" *she said, tucking a strain of her brown hair behind her ear.*

I handed her the pack and watched her light her cigarette with shaking hands.

"*Well, not, ask,*" *she said, playing with the door handle, then her purse strap, and finally pushing her glasses up her nose.* "*But, I just wanted to say, you're really pretty.*"

"*Ah, thank you.*" *I'd never been called pretty.* "*You are too.*"

She smiled in the awkward way of women who don't hear those words enough. "*Thank you, but you don't gotta say it back, ya know?*"

"*Oh, I know,*" *I said as my smile returned.*

As we entered my house, the tension between us was tangible. She was a beautiful woman, with mesmerizing eyes and a captivating smile. I couldn't help but feel drawn to her. Her brunette hair was pinned perfectly to her head, and her freckles on her nose were on full display making her milky skin even more inviting.

She kicked off her shoes, and I moved my eyes up her shapely calves to her muscular thighs, and I watched her watch me lick my lips.

"*You see anything you like?*" *she teased.*

"*Oh, most certainly.*" *I ran my eyes up the length of her body. She came closer and grabbed my hips bringing me in.*

I felt weak in her arms, and at first, I hated that sensation, but then her lips met mine and I lost the thought completely.

Her tongue parted my lips, and the taste of her last smoked cigarette was pleasurable. I felt her press her body into mine. But as the kiss deepened, I felt myself losing control. I didn't like the feeling of being consumed by desire or at the mercy of my emotions. So, with a sudden burst of willpower, I pulled away and got up from the couch.

"I'm going to make myself a drink," I said, my voice slightly shaky. I needed a moment to regain my composure before things went any further.

She looked at me with confusion and disappointment, but I couldn't bring myself to care. I needed to step back, to regain control of the situation before it spiraled out of hand.

"You okay?" she asked and I could actually hear the concern in her tone.

"Yeah, I'm cool. Just gonna get us some drinks."

"Okay."

As I made my way to the kitchen, I couldn't shake the guilt that washed over me. I knew I had to put a stop to it before it was too late. My fantasies were too strong, my thoughts beyond what she could give.

I took a long pull from the bottle, the liquid burning down my throat as I tried to calm my racing heart. I knew I had to do this, to cross the line between fantasy and reality. If

I didn't, I would be consumed by it. I wiped my mouth before taking another shot from the bottle, quietly went to my bedroom, and found my barbell, the only thing I could think of to make it quick. I didn't want to hurt her.

I just didn't want her to leave me.

"You got that drink yet?" she called from the couch.

"Yeah, I just had to check on the laundry."

"Oh, okay."

I walked up behind her, the barbell raised. She sat on the couch waiting for a drink that would never come.

Gripping the barbell, I licked my lips. My grip tightened on the cold metal. One second of self-doubt, and then I brought it down.

Hard.

My legs trembled as I felt the heavy steel smash into her skull, and my pants began sticking to me in the front. My knees buckled under the strength of my orgasm, and I nearly dropped the barbell.

She yelped like a kicked dog and flopped to the floor. I quickly walked around the couch and straddled her. I raised the barbell again and again. With each blow, I got more and more winded, yet the damage was growing. Blood shot out with each impact, flying from the wound, and slinging off the metal. My hands were covered in her blood, and I licked my lips where some had landed. Her screams faded, and her body fell still. I could see the life draining from her eyes as I continued my relentless attack.

The front of the couch was splattered, and the ceiling and walls were speckled with her blood. The carpet looked like a violent painting, and pockets still carried wet pools. The coffee table was shattered, and coated in the hitchhiker. My hands were dripping red, and my forearms were soaked in her remaining essence of this world. Streaks of crimson ran down my face, and it took everything in me not to keep swinging the barbell.

I had never felt such power, such control over another person. It was intoxicating, the way her body crumpled under my blows, the way her cries for mercy fueled my desire to keep going. I could feel the heat rising in my chest, the adrenaline coursing through my veins as I unleashed my pent-up fantasy on her.

Her skin was slick with sweat, her muscles tense and quivering as I brought the barbell down once more. The sound of bone cracking seemed to echo through the room, sending a shiver of pleasure down my spine. I leaned in close, my breath hot against her ear as I whispered, "You belong to me now."

And with that, I raised the barbell one final time, bringing it down with all the force I could muster. Her body went limp, her eyes staring blankly into the distance. I listened to the long exhale I knew was her last breath.

I stood over her, panting and sweating, a smile on my lips. My first real smile.

Dropping the barbell, I fell to my knees. Cupping my face in my hands, I began to cry.

What had I done?

I lay across her lifeless body, staring into her eyes. I breathed in the air around her, and my body quaked. My hand went underneath her dress, teasing her flesh, touching her legs. I pulled my lips in and stifled a moan. The fingers of my hand were no longer my own.

Her body, still warm, felt so good, nice, and needed.

I finally felt whole and complete.

Each touch intoxicated me, and stirred me, leaving me unable to protect my hidden desire any longer. Leaning in, my lips caressed hers. I kissed her slowly, yet deeply. My tongue entered her mouth, twirled around, and extracted itself so it could lick her lips one at a time. I traced her face with my tongue, framing her jaw with tender kisses, and my heart beat faster. I was shackled by euphoria. Feral desires magnified. Those deepest desires, the darkest ones, made me flush from needing to carry them out.

I made love to her.

I don't know how long I made love to her, but when I finally tried to stand, my legs buckled from weakness and I had to catch my balance on the couch. After the tremors of my orgasm subsided, I began to panic. What was I going to do with her body?

At first, I thought I was doing the right thing by hiding her body under the front porch. I was scared and panicked, not knowing what else to do. But as the night wore on, the weight of my actions began to weigh heavily on me. The thought of her lying there, under the house, where anyone could stumble upon her, made me paranoid and worried about every set of headlights that filtered in through my window blinds.

I couldn't sleep. Every creak of the floorboards, every rustle of the wind outside, made me jump, and think it was the police. I knew I had to do something, to do it quickly.

So, the next day, I took her body to the shed, where I had skinned the roadkill I collected. At first, the task made my stomach turn and my hands shake. But, soon, and very quickly, I fell in love with the smell, the sight, all my senses on high alert, and I grew aroused as I skinned her.

As I worked, tears streamed down my face. I couldn't believe what I was doing, what I had become so quickly. I had these fantasies and these dark dreams, but I never imagined myself capable of such cruelty, such violence. I couldn't even kill a deer when my dad took me hunting. But there was no turning back.

I still think about her every day. The guilt and shame of what I did will never leave me. But I hope, in some small way, by confessing, I have given her some measure of peace. And maybe, just maybe, I can find a way to forgive myself, too.

I sat naked on a turned-over bucket, pieces of Stephanie, dismembered and skinned, at my feet. I took the final draw from my cigarette as I stared at her bones with panicked joy. I was excited about what I was doing, but fearful of getting caught before I finished.

The sound of my heartbeat filled my ears as I stared down at the bones laid out before me. Feeling the weight of the hammer in my hand sent shivers down my spine, and made my thighs clench together. I took a deep breath, trying to steady my nerves as I raised the hammer above my head.

I brought it down with a force that sent a shock wave through my body. My entire arm vibrated, and it seemed to ripple through my shoulder. The bones shattered beneath the impact, splintering into pieces. Sharp cracks echoed through the room.

A rush of excitement coursed through me as I looked down at the broken fragments. The power I felt in this moment was intoxicating, a heady mix of fear and desire.

I continued to crush the bones, each blow sending a thrill through me. I could feel the heat building between my legs, a primal urge taking hold of me.

I don't know how long I stood there, lost in the frenzy of destruction, but when I finally stopped, my body trembled with need. Dropping the hammer, my chest heaved as I looked down at the shattered remains. I knew at that moment, I'd never be the same again.

Crushing the bones had awakened something dark and primal within me, and I couldn't wait to explore this newfound desire. Looking at the rest of the bones, my lips turned upward. I swung the hammer, cracking the bone in two, and shoved the jagged end into my mouth. Sucking, I could feel the spongy marrow enter my mouth, and I moaned. Twirling my tongue around my finger, I coated the marrow up to the knuckle, then, without hesitation, I shoved it into myself. Her innermost insides were now inside me, cementing her soul in my body.

I rode my own hand, grinding into my finger, wanting her deeper, and deeper within my very soul.

I cried out in orgasm and collapsed from the bucket. Shriving from the orgasmic vibrations, I thought of another way to have her with me. I gathered the bone powder and headed up to the balcony of the house. Standing on the balcony, covered in bone powder and lost in the throes of pleasure, I placed a kiss on the bone fragments in my hands before I scattered them into the night sky, watching as they drifted away on the wind.

· · · • · • · · ·

Club 219, the same club Dahmer frequented, now changed to the Wall Street Stock Bar. As I draw closer, my heart quickens, and my palms grow sweaty. I always love the hunt, searching, and finding.

I never drug the drinks. I only scout for the perfect girl. Sometimes, I am shut down, but other times, they are willing to have a friendly chat. It helps if they are a little conceited because it makes my photo shoot pitch more likely to be accepted.

Once inside, I'm dancing in the club, lost in the music and the lights. The beat is contagious, and I can't help but move my body to the rhythm. As I spin and twirl on the dance floor, I glimpse her.

She's stunning, with long, flowing hair and a smile that lights up the room. I can't take my eyes off her as she moves gracefully to the music. I feel a surge of nerves as I watch her, wondering if I should make a move.

Finally, as the night winds down, I muster up the courage to approach her. Walking over to where she's standing, I tap her on the shoulder. She turns to me, her eyes sparkling with curiosity.

"Hi," I say, trying to sound confident.

She smiles at me, and I feel a rush of relief. "Hi."

We dance together, and I can't believe my luck. She's even more beautiful up close, and her laughter is like music to my ears. We talk and laugh, and I feel like I've known her forever.

"Well, it's been fun, but I gotta get going."

"Okay," I say, trying to hide my anger before walking toward the bar.

I watch her leave, and just when I'm about to follow, an even more beautiful woman catches my eye, one moment forgotten for a new one.

A black-haired, glasses-wearing beauty orders a Manhattan. She has freckles on her nose and green eyes. I like her, and I want her.

So, I wait for her.

Watching her every move, my tongue swipes my lips.

She drinks her cocktail nice and slow, then gets up to put a song on the jukebox. She sways in her chair and dances to Norah Jones.

She wipes her mouth with the napkin from under her drink and gets up to leave. I follow her, watching as she walks toward Oregon Street.

I'm going against my normal routine by following her home, but I can't resist. She has this look about her, and I need to find out if she is different from the other girls. Something about her just screams, "It's me! I'm the one you've been searching for," and I can finally find out what I am missing.

······

"Daddy, Daddy, I made a game!"

"That's good, pumpkin," he said, looking at me briefly before returning his attention to the newspaper.

I ran over to his chair. "Daddy, do you wanna play with me?"

"Not right now." He didn't look away from his newspaper. "Maybe later."

Later never came, and never will.

Head down and shoulders slumped, I trudged to the one place I knew I wasn't alone. The one place I could just be myself without fear of judgment or ridicule.

I spent hours in my shed, surrounded by the bones of roadkill I had collected over the years. It may have seemed strange to some, but to me, they were a reminder of the fragility of life and the beauty that could be found even in death.

My board game was simple with only a few rules and the strategy of getting to the end without getting close to the other player's piece. I made the pieces out of bone and the board out of animal hide. My dad mentioned a smell when I began making it, but to me, it was a pleasant scent.

As I sat at the makeshift table in my shed, moving the pieces around the board and making decisions for both players, I almost forgot I was alone. Immersing myself in the game, losing track of time as I plotted my next move and tried to outsmart myself, I lost grip on my loneliness and felt happy.

But as the days turned into weeks and then months, the loneliness began to weigh on me. I longed for someone to share my creation with, to challenge me, and push me to think in new ways. But there was no one around who shared my interests.

My bones were my friends, and if I could just gather more I would have more friends to surround myself with, and then I wouldn't be lonely any longer.

· · · · · · · · · · ·

I linger behind as I follow her to her apartment building. It feels like an eternity, waiting for the perfect moment to make my presence known, yearning for a mere chance to say hello. My hands tremble and clutch the camera.

Every click, every snapshot holds the power to capture her essence, preserving it forever within the confines of my lens. I will have solid evidence to cherish and prove my theory that loneliness can be cured.

All of a sudden, she turns around and walks toward me.

"Hey, why the fuck have you been following me?" she asks while reaching into her purse.

"Sorry, I'm... I saw you leaving and thought you were beautiful. I didn't mean to creep you out. I've just been working up the nerve to ask if you want to be part of our photo shoot."

"Photo shoot?" Her face relaxes, and I can see the initial anger subsiding.

"Yeah, it's silly." I smile. "Just a commercial for athletic wear, and you are exactly the woman I envisioned for it."

She takes her empty hand out of her purse.

"So, where do we shoot this thing?"

"I have all my equipment at my apartment."

The memory of what I did last night comes back as I lead her to my apartment.

As I drilled into her head, I could hear her cries of pain and fear. But I pushed on, determined to see this through.

Finally, the drilling was done, and I waited for the transformation to occur. But as I looked into her eyes, I saw only confusion and fear. She was not the obedient zombie I hoped to create. Instead, she was a terrified and traumatized woman, trapped in a nightmare of my making.

It'd work this time though. It had to work eventually. It had to.

·········

I snap one last photo.

Capturing this moment for eternity.

Trapping this very instant forever.

Regardless of how the rest of the night plays out, she is mine now.

"See," I tell her with a smirk. "The camera loves you." I place the camera down after taking the film roll out of the back. Pointing at the roll I say, "That's for you if you want it."

Her self-loving personality makes her trusting and willing to show off her body so someone would compliment her. She is hungry for flattery, and savoring every acknowledgment of her beauty.

"See, I told you. Beautiful," I say.

"Thanks." She begins to gather her things to leave.

"Wait," I quickly call out. "Have a drink with me." I wait a second. "Please. You can even keep all the clothes you tried on."

"Okay, I can stay for a little while." She sits back down on the couch, putting her purse on the floor.

"So, you want a beer, or a rum and Coke?" I ask from the kitchen.

"A beer is fine."

"Coming up."

Returning to the living room, I hand her the glass of beer. I sit down and take a couple of sips before excusing myself to the bathroom. Once in the bathroom, I count to sixty before flushing the toilet and heading into my bedroom. The hammer I keep on my nightstand catches my eye, and I grasp it. I make my way behind her as I would if I was just coming back into the room normally so as not to raise her suspicion.

"So, what's your name?" I ask.

"Megan," she says. "And yours?"

She turns toward me.

With a swift motion, I swing the hammer, just as she looks up at me with a smile, its metal head connecting. The impact is vicious, the force of the blow turning her smile into a violent explosion of splintering bone. Shards of teeth flow through the air, falling to the floor like Game Show confetti. Megan cries out, blood running down her chin, and spits out the teeth that had fallen into her mouth.

Falling to the floor, she crouches and curls into a defensive ball. I yank her head up by the hair and smash the butt of the handle into her cheekbone. She fights and struggles, yet is too weakened by the initial blow to overpower me. I manage to get her back onto the couch, where I force her to look at me.

Her eyes plead for the same thing my heart pleads for: freedom. Freedom from the pain, from the anguish. Freedom from the never-ending gnawing at my soul.

The hammer swings once more into her face before I'm grappling with her, and fighting to get her clothes off. She struggles, but is weak and woozy, no doubt from the severe head trauma.

I waste no time gathering the photos, throwing the line of film across Megan's bare pussy. With a passion-filled determination, I begin driving the reel deep into her body with the hammer. With each thrust, the hammer's claw pierces the tender flesh of her vulva with a sickening sound reminiscent of sticking a finger in a jar of mayonnaise whenever the skin is torn, and colliding marbles whenever the metal connects to bone. There seems to be a sudden burst of energy from her, a fight for survival, and she fights to stand. I shove her back onto the couch, my hands gripping her shoulders tightly as I push her. I can see the fear in her eyes and I moan. The desire that burns within me is too strong, too overwhelming.

I crack her knees, the sound echoing through the room. The hammer, at first, sticks into her flesh from the force of the blow, but I yank it out. Crimson shoots out from the wound, and red droplets fling from the claw of the hammer as I raise it again, painting the walls with her blood. Moaning louder, I bring the hammer down again and this time the connection makes violent vibrations through my arm.

Using my other hand, I punch her in the throat with as much force as I can muster from the angle, but it's enough.

Her screams are muffled by the gurgles that escape her throat. I can see the pain in her eyes, the confusion, the fear. And I can't stop. I need her. I need to possess her completely.

I lean in close, my breath hot against her skin. I can feel her trembling beneath me. I can hear the rapid beat of her heart. I know she is scared, and this excites me even more. After one last peck on her tender lips, I continue my assault with the hammer, bringing it down on her legs and torso.

As I continue my relentless attack, something strange begins to happen. With each swoop of the hammer, the weight seems to lessen, as if it is no longer a mere tool, but a natural extension of my body. The hammer has become a penis, and I'm hitting her with loving taps and forceful thrusts. The tool has transformed into my erectile organ, and the twitching, writhing figure beneath me becomes my one and only love. She will never leave me, and I will make sure she will never try to.

Blood splatters across my face, mingling with the sweat that drips from my brow. At first, the gore had disturbed me, but now I see it for what it truly is.

The blood is our passion spent, our connection in liquid form.

With each strike, I feel power coursing through my veins. I revel in the control I have over Megan, the girl who had it all. Now, she is at my mercy, her body finally giving me that missing piece to complete me.

I drop the hammer and grab the Polaroid lying beside the other camera. I snap a photo, and as the picture rolls out I just can't hold back the urge any longer. I drop the camera and lower myself until my face is staring into her gaping and bloody pussy crater.

Leaning down, I bite firmly on the film and begin to pull out the strain of still images from her pussy. The strip is slick with blood and cum, ink, and busted bowels. I can see a piece of intestine poking out of her lower abdomen, and the stench of urine and shit is strong, but the smell of passion spent is the strongest. I am leaking, and getting wetter by the second. I just can't resist the urge to explore further.

I lick what is left of her clit, flicking my tongue across its maimed tip, and sucking on the puffy and scarred nub within the mass of brutalized meat. I rise up to admire her body.

Nervously, I put my hands on her damp flesh, exploring and touching every part, as if each piece is a separate work of art that I have to admire. Her breasts are barely a handful but fit perfectly in mine. Her nipples are pierced and hard. My fingers softly caress the dragonfly tattoo on her neck before making their way down the vines on her ribcage.

Slowly, I run my tongue up her neck and then I suck deeply on her soft throat, making myself tense with how slowly I am loving her. Forcing out a strong sound of arousal, I arch my back like a cat before licking her breasts and kissing her stomach.

Slipping my tongue in her navel I move it around as if trying to find a way inside her. I am becoming wet with anticipation.

Moving down, as my body quivers, I lick and suck at the inner part of her tender thigh. Sliding my tongue across her skin, I open that space between her thighs and unlock it with my tongue. Her neatly trimmed mound tickles my chin gently as I explore her depths. I begin painting the walls of her sex. Legs trembling, muscles tense, I take one deep breath of the coppery scent mingling with her natural odor before I swipe her opening as if licking the frosting off of a cupcake.

Jolts of electricity roll through my body creating tiny earthquakes of pleasure that continue to build the overwhelming sensation of a forthcoming orgasm. I make circles with my tongue, catching as much of her blood as I can, and dart it in and out. I bite down on the flap of skin that hangs from the left of the messy wound, the part most brutalized by the hammer, and then I cry out in orgasm as her juices fill my mouth.

Each mouthful oozes out of my pooched lips. I find myself helpless to the sensation. I begin to knuckle under the inviting flavor of each mouthful. The pieces of her flesh seem to dance on my tongue, masking the numbing reality that encases my existence. With each bite, the weight of my depression grows lighter. I truly feel I am one step closer to finding that missing piece of myself. Each chew serves as a key to unlock the emptiness that consumes me.

In the depths of my passion, I cling desperately to the fragile belief that somehow, a single bite more will restore what is lost within me. With each mouthful I devour, a fleeting glimmer of hope ignites deep within me. I pray that I can momentarily bridge the vast gap between emptiness and fulfillment, but with each bite I swallow, my mouth left bare and empty, the painful truth unfurls before me.

My face is fully submerged inside her. Blood leaks around my ears as I push deeper, and continue to take chunks of her out with my teeth.

I am stuck in an insatiable cycle, a cruel dance that weaves together fleeting moments of satisfaction with an unending yearning, perpetually leaving me longing for just one more bite. Each swallow seems to mock me, confirming the inevitable truth that I am forever bound to this relentless pursuit of happiness, a hungriness that gnaws at the very core of my soul, incessantly taunting me with its ceaseless demands for completion.

I know I have sunk deeper and deeper into the abyss, but I remain locked within this relentless struggle, unable to break free from the grips of my own desperation.

As the cycle relentlessly repeats, the realization dawns upon me like a harsh dash of ice-cold water across my face. This search, this insatiable hunger, is slowly devouring my very essence, leaving nothing but a hollow shell behind. In wanting to create a zombie, I myself have been turned into one.

All of a sudden, a loud knocking comes from the door.

"Police! Open up! Police!"

·········

They ask me when I first thought of killing someone. They also ask how old I was when I first thought of taking someone's life.

It was the summer of my sophomore year before school started back, and my dad and I were out on the lake fishing. It was a tradition we started when I was just a little kid and something I always looked forward to, even though we never talked much. It was a time that he was actually there with me, seeing me, instead of ignoring me.

As we sat in the boat, the sun beating down on us, I couldn't help but feel a sense of peace. The water was calm, the birds were chirping, and the only sound was the gentle lapping of the waves against the boat and the occasional cough from him while he smoked his cigarette.

My dad and I didn't talk much as we fished. I was thankful for that because I didn't have the words to truly describe what was going on in my head lately. My mind was so full of these confusing thoughts and I tried to just focus on what he taught me about fishing, from how to bait a hook to how to reel in a big catch.

As the day wore on, we caught a few fish here and there, but mostly, we just enjoyed the quiet. "See, here," my dad explained, "you slice it here, but not too close. You don't want to cut into the intestines. You see?"

"Yeah." I was excited, watching my dad cut into the fish's stomach.

Sunlight sparkled on the pile of scales we'd removed, and its eyes seemed to stare accusingly at my dad. Yet, its innards called out to me.

As he made the first incision, a smell filled the air. My dad held his face in the 'something stinks' grimace, but I thought it was pleasant. There was a tingling, a subtle yet powerful feeling that I couldn't explain growing within my groin. As he was starting to carefully remove the guts, I felt a heat radiate between my thighs.

"Can I try?"

"Sure, just be careful."

He handed me the knife and the fish. I followed his instructions. I slit cautiously and began to pull on the intestines. The fish's insides were slimy and slippery, my thighs clenched, and the heat grew more intense but I didn't understand what it truly was and why.

That's when I had my first thought.

What do our insides look like? How do they feel? Would I also be attracted to them?

And then, the darkest thought came: How would I get away with it?

· · · · · · · · · ·

As I sit in the frigid interrogation room, my heart heavy with guilt and fear, I pick up the phone and use my one call to dial my dad's number. The anticipation builds with each ringing tone until finally, his voice answers on the other end. The words catch in my throat like lumps of half-chewed food as I struggle to find the courage to speak.

"Dad, I, uh," I begin, my voice quivering with emotion.

"Yes?" his voice wavers slightly as if he already knows.

"I did, uh, I did something bad." The weight of those words hangs heavily in the air, the silence between us deafening.

"How bad is it this time?"

"There's no forgiving me, Dad. I killed people."

There's a sharp intake of breath on his end before he responds, his voice thick with emotion. "I... I'm so sorry, pumpkin," he stammers, the words oozing with guilt. "I failed you. I should have been there for you more. I know, I should've done better..."

"It wasn't you, Dad. I don't blame you. Uh, I, I only blame myself, really."

"I blame me."

"Don't do that, Dad. This was my own fault."

Tears threaten to spill from my eyes as his words wash over me like a tidal wave, a tsunami of regret and sorrow as if I am in the eye of the storm fighting every emotion all at once. I can hear the pain in his voice, the burden of responsibility crashing into his heart like a truck.

Through the phone line, my regret and fear meet his guilt and sorrow.

For once in my life, we're connected.

But, I know I am still a monster, in fact, I've known for a long time.

·········

I took her to the Ambassador Hotel, a luxurious and indulgent setting for our evening of passion. As soon as we shut the door to our room, we couldn't keep our hands off each other. We both quickly undressed and kissed. The anticipation and desire had been building all night, and now we were finally alone.

"Slow down," I said as I pushed her hands down from my hips. "Let me make you a drink."

"Okay," she said, drawing it out like a spoiled brat not getting her way.

With my back to her, I dashed some liquor into the glasses, and slyly slipped a few sleeping pills into one of them, intending to put her to sleep so she wouldn't feel any pain.

I handed her one of the glasses and took a sip of my own.

Oh fuck, *I thought,* I don't remember if I gave her the right one or not. Shit.

The effects were almost immediate, and I felt myself growing dizzy and disoriented. My eyes were fighting to stay open, and the room was spinning.

"Are you okay?" she asked in the haze of my vision.

"I'm good. I'm good."

"You don't look good." She put her drink down and held on to my swaying body.

Anger and frustration boiled inside me as I realized my error. I lashed out, my fists connecting with her delicate features. The room spun around me as I unleashed my rage, unable to control my actions. I honestly hadn't planned on killing her, but it was happening.

"What the fuc-" she said, holding her face as I tackled her to the ground, and straddled her.

I hit her in the face over, and over. Holding her face still with my other hand, I forced her to look at me. I stared into her eyes and basked in the total control I had over her. She bucked and kicked out, but I had my full weight pressed into her chest and pinned down in place. She was under my full submission, and I had absolute power over her.

I kept smashing my fist into her face, the feeling of her teeth cutting my knuckles only fueling my lust. I could see the fear in her eyes, but it only made me want her more.

I needed this.

I needed to have this moment.

I grabbed a pair of panties from the floor and began shoving them between her lips, forcing her mouth open, and stuffing the silk down her throat. Her choking and struggles only made me wetter.

I watched as her eyes went blank and her body went limp. I kissed her cheek, and gently breathed in her last breath as if it were an inhale from a cigarette.

And then, as she lay before me, still, soundless, and lifeless, yet warm, I knew it was time to take things to where I wanted them to truly go.

She's mine.

I licked her breast and kissed her stomach as if I were afraid of getting caught. My eyes searched hers as I slipped my tongue inside her navel, searching for her satisfaction before I slid it up and out of her belly button.

I fingered her as I massaged a nipple, then massaged her ass, giving each cheek a playful spank, a sting, then pulled her hair, turned her face toward me, kissed her, saw she was okay and kissed again.

Again, my tongue went toward her. I adjusted her body, and directed her sex, as I wiggled my tongue inside her innermost part. I held both of her legs up, pushed them back over her head, her ass high in the air, like she was in some kind of yoga pose. I licked and suckled. I trembled. My body heated up more and more with each stroke of my tongue. I imagined flames coming out of my pores to engulf her.

The taste of her on my lips only added to the intensity of the moment, and I found myself lost in a haze of pleasure unlike anything I had ever experienced.

My hands cupped her ass, fingers digging into the soft flesh, and I felt my nipples harden and grow sore from the tautness of arousal. That hurt so good. I savored her. Made myself squirm, beg, and fall madly in love with this moment in time. Made me feel like all this was worth it, as long as I could have this moment again and again.

When my tongue was inside her, I felt as bright as a burning star, and when I stopped, I felt the darkness dip into my soul. I needed this. When I slipped away from what I felt were the edges of pure love, I forced myself to keep licking until it was time once more to feel the heat of the star grow.

The star grew hotter, and hotter, until finally, it exploded, and the light was no more. My orgasm shook the room. My entire body was hot, and burning with pain. It hurt so good to feel such a powerful orgasm explode from me. My thighs were glued together by cum, and the skin of my legs was squishing in the wet carpet I had drenched in my downpour as I trembled and shivered in the aftershocks of my climax.

As I finally collapsed beside her, my body spent and my mind reeling, I knew that I had found my true climax. And as I drifted off to sleep, my legs wrapped around her lifeless frame, and my face nuzzling her shoulder, I knew that I would never be satisfied with anything less than the darkest, most twisted pleasures imaginable.

I turned my head and stared into her eyes, and in that moment, I couldn't help but think to myself, I am a monster.

· · · • · • · · ·

As the new inmates shuffle through the intimidating gates of the prison, the harsh reality of their situation sinks in. The uniformed guards bark orders, their faces hardened by years of dealing with the incoming waves of inmates.

The processing area is a chaotic mess of noise and tension. Women of all ages and backgrounds huddle together. The air is thick with the scent of disinfectant and the stale stench of unwashed bodies.

I hear some of the women talking behind me.

"Is that her?"

"Yeah, that's her."

It doesn't surprise me that they know. Even in prison, the inmates are allowed to watch the news, and I made the headlines in all the papers and stations.

"Do you think it's true?"

"Oh, fuck yeah. She fucking did it."

Standing nervously, my heart pounding in my chest, I clutch a small bag of belongings, the only remnants of my former life that the jail let me keep. As I move forward in line, the reality of my situation begins to sink in.

A guard barks orders at me, his voice cutting through the chaos. "Name?" he demands, his eyes cold and indifferent. "Never mind, I fuckin' know you."

The guard scribbles something on a form and motions for me to step forward. I hear him mutter, 'Fucking sicko', as I am directed to a nearby table where another prison officer searches through my belongings, confiscating anything deemed contraband, which, by the looks of it, is everything. He throws out my Bible, which my grandmother had given me, my first letter from my father while I awaited trial and even my address book with my father's phone number inside. I called him every week but was never any good at remembering the number.

Feeling exposed and vulnerable, I fight to keep my composure. Lingering on the women around me, my gaze travels along each woman carrying their own burden of shame and regret, yet each one looks at me, knowing me from the news, and judging me. *I deserve this.* I know they all think I'm a monster. *I am a monster.* The officer dumping my entire life in the trash was telling me without words, I am garbage.

Finally, the processing is complete, and I am led to another room that takes me into the main hall. As I glance back at the chaos of the processing area, I know that my life will never be the same once I cross that threshold.

I am right where I deserve to be.

Through the heavy metal doors, I am ushered into a world devoid of hope and suffused with an overwhelming sense of despair, deeper than any loneliness I've ever felt.

Is this real?

The walls seem to breathe, exhaling sadness as the cold air clings to my lungs. The harsh lights flicker above, casting an eerie glow over the hallways, even more confusing than the ones at my apartment during my first month there. This is my new reality, where time slips away, leaving nothing but the weight of remorse and regret.

I deserve this, I deserve death for what I have done. Even this hell is too good for me. Unfortunately, Wisconsin doesn't give the death penalty so I am forced to live out the rest of my life locked in this concrete madhouse.

Seventeen life sentences.

A seemingly infinite stretch of existence reduced to a mere number, etched on my inmate profile. The judge's gavel fell, sealing my fate. Life outside is retreating like a distant memory. The world moves on, leaving me locked within this timeless box.

I still hear the sister of my second to last victim, the deaf girl I picked up at the bar one night, screaming in the courtroom, *'I fucking hate you! You! You fucking hear me! Goddamn it, look at me, mother fucker!'*.

A hushed anticipation hangs heavily in the air, as I shuffle down the hallway with a guard following me.

"You know, you ain't gonna be gettin' no special treatment here. You're gonna go in the dog pen with the rest of 'em." I hear the guard's second chin flapping as she tells me this.

The silence is shattered by the single cracking blow of a clenched fist meeting flesh.

"Get that bitch!"

"Fuck that sick fuck up!"

I turn around to look for the guard, but she is no longer there. It is true. I was thrown in the dog cage without any aid or help at all.

My ears fill with the pressure of her punches. Blood sprays in violent arcs, and paints the concrete wall-turned-canvas, splattering like grim strokes of a dark artist. My teeth clatter against my jaw. My head is spinning, and my vision is blurry and fading. Everything is dim, and then...

It all goes black.

·‥•●•‥·

Hands shaking, my naked body cold, I opened the box, my heart pounding with anticipation. Inside, her decapitated head stared back at me, her eyes wide and unblinking. Reaching inside, I gently picked it up, feeling a strange mix of excitement and unease. I didn't want to get caught by my Grandma. I look at the door to make sure I locked it.

I couldn't resist the urge to kiss her, to feel her lips against mine. I knew that pleasure wasn't happiness, but pleasure made me feel happy, and less alone, at least while it was happening. I breathed on her neck, and blew a stream of air to help cool myself off, but only stoked the fire within me. I shuddered and began to utter feeble cries to give myself more. Caressing her face, I dragged my fingers across her soft cheek. Tingles spread. I felt it rising and rising within me. Orgasm called out my name, but eluded me.

My tongue brushed the inside of her mouth, playing with her tongue. I ran my tongue across her teeth and moaned as a tooth scraped the tip. Her mouth was dry but quickly became wet from my salivating mouth. Her lips were soft, and stiff, but felt how I always imagined a kiss would feel.

The suddenness of her mouth on my sex surprised me. When did I place her mouth on me? *Her mouth, the musical way her lips strummed my chord, the perfect way she massaged the right spot made me set free blissful moans, sing out to the very night, and float and fly. As I moaned, I rubbed my clit with slow strokes.*

I was in a state so intense, so extreme, that I was beyond reason and self-control. Tears of pleasure clouded my vision, closing my eyes, I drowned in the sensations. I cried out in orgasm, and as the orgasm diminished, a new orgasm started growing and my body shook with the power of it sprouting from my very core. My legs trembled, and a puddle of cum drenched my bed and soaked her hair.

I held on to her head like I never wanted her to leave. Beads of sweat on my flesh. Beads of cum on hers. Our skin sticking together. We were one.

For tonight, we were one.

Then I wake up in my cell, body saturated with sweat as I remember that night in my room, reliving the moment of connection I felt.

Looking at the steel door, and feeling the cold metal beneath me that serves as my bed, my eyes cloud once more, but not from tears of pleasure, these were tears of pain and sorrow.

··········

The first night in solitary confinement is the worst, as the reality of my confinement begins to set in. They tell me they are only doing this for my protection. They refuse to listen when I tell them it doesn't matter. But as always, the officers win and I am forced into a protective custody cell. Sleep becomes a distant acquaintance, elusive and fleeting, as the weight of the steel door presses upon my mind like a full set of weights. My face hurts and is swollen.

I deserve this.

Hopes and dreams wither and die, their fragile petals crushed beneath the grindstone of my reality. Love, once a distant memory, becomes an elusive dream. Boundaries disappear, and time becomes a shapeless blur.

Days turned into weeks, weeks into months, as the monotonous routine of prison life settles in. Marking each day inside the back of the Bible my father bought me to replace my grandmother's, as if I am tallying up a scorecard, I manage to keep track of the days.

I start getting mail from people I don't know. At first, it is only one or two every week, and then I start getting five or six a week. They write to me as if they know me, and it is calming to think some people actually care about my well-being and the healing of human connection.

My face heals, and I am once again able to chew my food without wincing in pain. The constant clang of officer's keys, the slamming steel doors, and the whispered conversations that vanish into the void become the soundtrack to my existence.

Suddenly, a knock at my door blasts through my cell, and wakes me from my nap.

"Mail call!" the officer yells as he shoves a stack of letters through the trap in the middle of the door.

One card reads: *'The compulsion became stronger and the obsession more intense, it became the main focus of my life.'* with a little drawing of a cannibal on the front wearing big glasses. I open it, and the lady had written in big block letters: WAY TO GO, LADY DAHMER! YOU'RE A MASTER CHEF, HUH? HOW ABOUT SHARING YOUR SECRET SAUCE!

I snort as I put the card on my bed and open one from another young woman. This letter is written in beautiful cursive, and says, 'I've been to prison. If you ever get lonely, I'll let you eat me.'

Letter after letter, I open, and I'm shocked by each one. They are full of money, stamps, one-liners, and half-naked photos. These women seem to love me for what I have done. I don't deserve their love, but it is hard not to let the feeling of being accepted wash over me.

Are these women for real? I think. *Do they really love me? Do they really accept me?*

· · · • • • • • · ·

"Hey, Dahmer!" a kid called out while I walked to my first-period class.

"Yes?" My annoyance was apparent because I didn't like the fact this was my second year of freshman math as it was, and I definitely didn't feel like putting up with more jokes, but then again it was my only way to interact with people.

"Do the Dahmer, man," he shouted, trying to gain more attention on me, "Do the Dahmer."

The Dahmer was a thing I started to do a few months ago. I had been really drunk and bored in the classroom. I tried to take notes and listen, but in all actuality, I could have cared less about anything she was teaching. There was this mentally challenged kid in my fourth-period class who suffered from Tourette's, and so I just started acting as if I was having a seizure and a stroke mixed with a little of their Tourette's.

"Dah, duh, dah," I cried out with shaking hands, and drool coming out of my mouth. "Dah, duh, dah."

I dropped to the ground and rolled a few times, and all the kids laughed, and in that moment, I was liked. But, once the moment was over, I was nothing more than a phantom once more.

I'd walk down the halls and hear the other kids whisper.

"Oh god, Jessie, don't turn around, the freak is behind you."

"Shit! Don't let her make eye contact with me. Fucking freakazoid."

Jessie was a girl I had tried talking to once, but it didn't go well.

"Hey Jessie," I had said, trying to catch her after biology class.

"Yeah?" Just looking at her face, you'd know we never spoke before.

"Um...um, well you like biology, right?"

"Yeah?" she said nice and slow, drawing out the confusion in her tone.

"Um...would you...um...would you like to come back to my place?"

"Your place?"

"Yeah. I...I...um...I got some roadkill we could dissect and practice and..."

"Eww, no!" she whispered and kept walking away as if she had never spoken. "That's fucking gross."

I watched her walk away, and go to her friends. They pointed at me and shook their heads. Knowing I was now just a joke to them, I walked away, left school, and went to my shed.

My shed was my safe place. Inside I wasn't alone. I was surrounded by my friends.

I ran my finger across the bone fragments and the rotting carcass of a raccoon I had found on the road a few miles from home. The feeling of its open body warmed my hand and made me close my eyes in pleasure. I fingered its tiny heart, rubbed down its still slimy tissue, and thought of just how much I would like to know how it would feel inside me.

I lacked any real connection with my peers because I was different. I didn't fit in with the popular crowd or the outcasts. I was just... there. A ghost in the halls of my high school, invisible to everyone except those who wanted to make fun of me.

Sitting in class, I cracked a beer open and just started drinking. Each sip of beer numbed the pain more and more, until the taste of beer was all I could focus on, and the pain was forgotten. Finishing the first beer, I cracked open another one and licked the foam off my fingers.

I bought the beer with stolen money I would take from Mom's purse or sometimes Dad's wallet when he was home long enough to give me the opportunity, but I never felt bad about it, because it made the pain go away. I was never carded because I looked old for my age.

"What are you doing?" the teacher called out.

"It's my medicine," was always my answer as I took another swig of my medicine and let out a loud belch.

· · · ● ● · ● ● · · ·

After dropping off a few letters at the blue mailbox outside the nurse's station, I walk toward the chow hall. It's lunch, and believe it or not, writing all those responses had worked up my appetite.

The chow hall, a dimly lit room, is adorned with worn tables and benches. Plastic cutlery echoes throughout the hall, bouncing off plastic trays, the only rhythm to be found that breaks the monotony. The food, a pitiful attempt, lays on the trays like a slap in the mouth. It is tasteless slop, devoid of flavor, served as a cruel joke that forces you to spend money at the canteen.

The guards, ever watchful, survey the scene with detached indifference. They don't care if you are a child molester, a rapist, or a girl who only bagged a few stolen items from a shopping mall, to them we are all pieces of shit.

At each table I pass, I can hear the whispers about me.

"Oh, god, that's her."

"She doesn't look like a killer."

"Fucking sicko."

"Fucking sick ass motherfucker!"

I sit down at an empty table. Today's lunch is supposed to be pot pie but is instead crust-less slop with bits of chicken-looking mystery meat. Staring at the empty table spots before me, I pick up a long strain of the meat and stare at it a moment before showcasing it in the air.

"You know? This is what veins sometimes look like!" I shout. My fans think things like this are funny, so I am hoping I can make a couple of girls laugh and maybe even make a friend.

But instead, I only get more insults.

"Shut the fuck up, sicko."

"Fuck you, Dahmer!"

"Fucking nasty ass fuck."

I dump my tray and go back to my cell. At least in my cell, I have friends. I pick up another stack of letters, and once again, I'm welcomed with fan mail.

· · · ● · ● · · · ·

The next day after breakfast, while walking to the library I am stopped by a young black girl.

"You fucking disgust me, Dahmer," she says spitting in my face. "I am a God-fearing Christian and I know you'll have to pay for your sins."

"I'm sorry," I say, wiping my face.

"I am tired of your disrespect. You don't deserve to fucking live."

"I know that," I say. "I asked them to kill me, and they gave me nine hundred years instead."

Shaking her head, she says, "Then start fucking acting like it. This shit ain't no game, bitch."

The girl gives me a gentle shove and walks away. Feeling more alone with each passing second, I go into the library to clear my head.

The library is more of a hangout for couples, and gangs than an actual library, but it's a place to clear your head and find whatever book you need to take you away from the reality of prison. At first, I picked up a copy of *Gothic Filth* by Asher Dark, but I just read it last week, so even though I could easily read it again, I put it down. Picking up *Rural Decay* by Jason Nickey, I go check out and go back to my cell.

·········

Looking at another stack of fan mail, I can't shake the feeling of shame. *I deserved this. I deserved this more than anyone.*

Each piece of fan mail only serves to solidify that I am a monster. They praise me, awe over me, and I know deep down that I don't deserve it. I only deserve to be alone.

Opening another letter and reading the first line, I let out a sigh before dropping the letter to the floor. I repeat this three more times before I find a letter from my dad in the stack.

"Dear pumpkin," it read. "You know I love you. Well, that didn't come out right on paper. I love you, pumpkin. I will always love you. Regardless of what you have done, you are my daughter. One of the family's mothers approached me the other day and asked me if I forgave you. I thought it was crazy that she had forgiven you really, I mean I don't know if I'd be able to in her position, but she said it was the Lord who told her to. That got me thinking, I am sorry I never.... I never baptized you. I never took you to church, and maybe if I'd taken the time, maybe you wouldn't have been driven away from Christ and into the Devil's hands. Do you go to the church there? Or it's called a chapel, isn't it? Do you have the Bible I sent you? Please read it so you can start to seek His salvation. I just don't want you to go to Hell. No matter what, you are worthy of the glory of heaven. Your Dad."

In the last week, I have now heard about God two different times from two different people. Was this a coincidence or one of those mysterious miracles?

· · • • · • • • · ·

Once convinced by my gentle persuasion, she agreed to come back to my place. As I welcomed her inside, I told her, "I live with my grandma, so please be quiet."

"Yeah, sure thing," she smiled.

I poured a couple of mugs of coffee, trying to create a comfortable atmosphere for her to relax and unwind.

"So, what do you do?"

"I'm a photographer," I said. "I also do taxidermy."

"Taxidermy? That's wild. I've always wanted to just watch that happen, just out of curiosity, really."

"You wanna see what I'm working on now?"

"Really?"

"Yeah, really." I smiled. "Follow me."

Leading her to the door to the basement, we walked down the stairs, both trying to remain as quiet as we could.

"It's actually pretty interesting," I said.

"I bet. It's always been a subject on my to-do list." Her laugh was beautiful. She was beautiful. Everything about

her was beautiful, her face, her arms, her legs, her voice, everything.

"This is it," I said as I opened the cabinet. "These are the tools, and this is...." I picked up a hammer. "This is how you get into the skull."

"Wow, it seems very violent." Her lips turned upward, and she leaned in closer. "Oh, a radio," she said as she turned it on.

The moment became slow motion, her lips touched mine and her tongue parted my lips. The Shirelles sang 'Baby It's You' softly as we kissed.

Tongues danced a slow, unhurried dance. We kissed endlessly.

Her hand moved to my breasts, touched with gentle pressure, and then her finger circled the nipple through the fabric of my shirt. Her hand moved down my body and settled on the small of my back. I pulled my bottom lip in, bit down, and tried to ignore the fire beginning to burst below.

My eyes went to hers, her passion, her intense stare, and I knew I couldn't match that level of emotion. Uncomfortable, I closed my eyes. She kissed my face over and over, her kisses patient and telling of a need deeper than just sex.

Tears were in my eyes. So many tears. She was teasing me, controlling me just like everyone else. Forcing me to think of things I didn't want just like everyone else. She was just like the rest of them.

Stop it, *I thought,* just stop it.

I shoved her, and charged her, all in one motion. We crumbled to the ground, and before she could yell, or cry out, I swung the hammer into her skull. She made a single loud exhale and was out cold.

Standing up, I walked to the cabinet and pulled the hacksaw off the corkboard. I stood over her, straddling her, and stared into her face. Why did you have to do that? Why did you have to make me feel small and worthless? Powerless, just like everyone else has. Why?!

I got down to her level, and touched her gently with the saw's blade before I said out loud, "You're with me now."

As I gripped the saw tightly in my hands, I could feel the vibrations coursing through my arm as it bit into the flesh with a crunch. Blood sprayed out, coating my hands and arms in a sticky, warm liquid. My lips moved upward and I kept sawing, trying not to think about how I might wake Grandma. Bobby Darin sang 'Mack the Knife' as I admired her body.

The sound of the saw cutting through flesh was like soft sighs, drowning out any other thought in my head. The sigh from the saw reminded me of the same sighs that escape during my orgasms. I could feel the resistance as I pushed harder, the blade slicing through the tough tissue with each back-and-forth motion. The smell of blood and sweat filled the air, making my head spin with a mixture of arousal and urgency.

I glanced up briefly, meeting the gaze of her lying before me. Her eyes were closed, her chest rising and falling rapidly as I sawed. I could feel the beads of sweat forming on my forehead, my body trembling with exhilaration. Her rapid rising and falling chest stopped rising and stopped falling, and my heart sped up as I watched it happen.

I leaned in closer, my breath hot against her skin as I continued to saw through the flesh. The sight of the blood glistening on her skin only fueled my desire, sending tiny sparks of pleasure from my fingertips to my whole body. I could feel the heat building between my legs, an urge taking over as I basked in the power I held over her now.

With one final push, the saw cut through the bone with a satisfying snap. I pulled back, panting heavily as I admired the unveiled beauty. The sight of the severed limb lying before me sent a rush of fantasies through my mind, a sense of satisfaction washing over me, knowing I could do it.

Dropping the saw, and leaning in to grab her arm, I was also trying to unbutton my pants with the other hand as fast as I could.

Pants down, arm in hand, I used her like a back-scratcher, placing her hand on me, moving my hand holding her arm, her hand gliding over me wherever I put it.

I lay in the pool of gore, sliding her arm over me, and rubbing her blood up and down my vagina. I coated my clit with the warm stickiness and flicked the tip of it before sliding one of her fingers into me.

As I moaned and made blood angels on the floor, my hips wiggled into her arm. My orgasm built quicker, and quicker, until eventually I cried out and came all over her hand. I loosened my grip on her arm, and it fell beside me with a wet thump. I leaned in and kissed the end that I had severed from. The flesh tickled my lips and teased my tongue as I began to lick the threads of sawed flesh.

I lay there and breathed her in. She was all mine.

She was all mine.

I'm not sure how long I laid with her, but eventually, I knew I had to clean up and go upstairs, so I did.

"Good morning," Grandma said as she sat at the table with her Bible and tea. "You been down there all night?" she asked as I stepped into the kitchen.

"Morning, Grandma," I said as I fixed the coffee pot.

With a gentle smile, my grandma sat me down at the kitchen table and said, "My dear girl, I've noticed that you seem a bit uncomfortable in social situations. You come in late and spend all that time downstairs alone. Have you considered joining our community church group? It might help you feel more connected and overcome your shyness."

Unsure of how to respond, I fidgeted with my hands and tucked a strand of hair behind my ear. Finally, I spoke up in my soft voice as I took a sip of coffee. "But Grandma, I'm not sure if the church is the right place for me. I feel more at peace here."

She nodded understandingly, realizing my uniqueness was not something to be changed but embraced. With a warm smile, she said, "I love you just the way you are. You know that. Just think about it, dear."

"Thank you, Grandma. I will"

· · • • • • • • • · ·

Is Dad right, I think as I hold his letter. *Do I need to find Christ? To find God?*

Placing his letter on the table, I decide to head up to the chapel after the chow call.

Chow comes and goes, and I'm on my way to the chapel, rubbing my hands together, and sweating. I know my nervousness is on full display.

Once inside, I knock on the Chaplain's door and ask if I can talk to him.

"Yes, come on in." He waves at the empty chair in front of him. I sit, cross, and uncross my legs before getting up the nerve to ask my question. "Dahmer? Yes?"

"Yeah." I bite my lip and adjust my glasses. "That's me." I finally look up into his eyes, and to my surprise they are kind.

"Can God still forgive me, even with what I've done?" I ask, my voice trembling with fear and longing for redemption.

The Chaplain looks into my eyes and smiles. "God's mercy knows no bounds," he says gently. "You read the Bible? I mean really read it?" He laughed as if he already knew the answer.

"No, not like I should."

"There's a story for those that speak to me that I feel like you need to hear. It's the story of Saul on the road to Damascus. It is about finding where you are, and leading yourself to where you need to be."

"Where is that?"

He picks a Bible up from his desk, and with his liver-spotted hand, he hands it to me. "That's up to you to find out, Dahmer. It will take you truly taking the time to let God show you that and for you to truly be honest with yourself. No one is beyond redemption, and no one is too broken. You'll see when you read it."

Tears well up in my eyes as I feel a glimmer of hope in my darkness. I never dared to believe that forgiveness was possible for someone like me. "But can I ever make amends for what I've done?" I whisper, my voice barely audible.

The Chaplain reaches out and takes my hand, his wrinkled skin surprisingly soft and gentle, and offers a comforting squeeze. "You can start by accepting what you have done and using whatever time you have left to bring light into this world. It won't be easy, but with faith and genuine remorse, you can find salvation."

"I am sorry for what I've done. I know it doesn't make it right."

"No, it isn't right, but the first step is to accept that it's wrong."

"Okay," I say as I hang my head briefly before looking back at him. His calm blue eyes seem to cast a cloud of empowerment over me, and I truly believe I can overcome this, and find salvation.

· · · · · ● · · · ·

Once I am back in my cell, I start thinking about what the Chaplain told me about how God could be my guide, companion, and friend, wash away my sins, and give me a clean slate to be normal.

I never thought I would find comfort in a stolen mannequin, but here I was, sneaking it upstairs to my room while Grandma slept soundly in hers. I knew it was wrong to steal it, but I couldn't help but feel a sense of companionship when I lay next to it in my bed.

As I settled in next to the mannequin, becoming its big spoon, a rush of excitement ran through my entire body and settled in that pit in the center of me igniting a flame. In that moment, it wasn't just a hunk of molded plastic, it was a true companion. It was mine. It was all mine, and I was in control of it. I started to caress its smooth plastic surface, feeling a sense of connection. Grinding my hips into it, wrapping my leg around it so I could get perfect friction, I imagined that the mannequin was a real person. In that moment, it felt like I had found a solace that I had been missing for so long. The forbidden nature of the act only added to the thrill.

I reached out tentatively, my fingers grazing the smooth surface of its arm. What felt like an ice cube ran down my spine as I imagined what it would feel like if this mannequin was real, where it might touch, kiss, and caress. Without thinking, I began caressing its body, tracing the curves and contours with my hands. I placed my lips gently on its throat. Each kiss played in slow motion as I pressed down with pressure.

As I continued to explore the mannequin's form, a wave of desire washed over me like a giant wave from an ocean's storm. I closed my eyes and let myself get lost in the fantasy, imagining that this inanimate object was a real person, eager for my touch as much as I was eager for its touch.

I knew it was not real, a delusion maybe, but in that moment, it felt like I had found a kind of solace that I had been missing for so long. The forbidden nature of the act only added to the thrill, sending a rush of adrenaline through my veins. I felt so powerful, so strong. I had sneaked it past Grandma and claimed it as my own. It was mine, and it belonged to me.

I couldn't help but moan softly as I pleasured myself, even though I was fighting to be quiet. I was too lost in the illusion of companionship that the mannequin provided. The room faded away, leaving only me and this perfect, controllable figure.

I came closer to the edge.

Closer.

And, closer.

Almost there.

Finally, as I reached the peak of ecstasy, I opened my eyes and looked at the mannequin before me. Its blank, expressionless face seemed to mock me, reminding me of the reality of the situation.

Cum glided down my finger, and with it, the dream also slid away from my consciousness. I shared my final moan of pleasure with no one.

What if God could give me the companionship I need?

I want to believe.

I need to believe.

I will believe.

I do believe.

· · • • • • • • · ·

Sitting in my cell, tracing my dad's letter with my fingertip, my mind wanders to when I tried to tell him about myself.

"Dad, can I talk to you?"

"Sure," he said as he turned a page in his newspaper.

"Dad, can we talk about something important?" I asked tentatively, trying to muster up the courage to broach the subject weighing heavily on my mind.

"Sure, what's on your mind, kiddo?" he replied, looking up from his newspaper, and setting it down. The annoyance in his tone was apparent, but I needed to talk to someone.

"I... I wanted to talk to you about..." I said, my voice barely above a whisper. "About how I feel... I feel different."

My dad's expression faltered for a split second before he quickly regained his composure. "Oh, that's nothing to worry over, pumpkin."

I felt a surge of relief wash over me, thinking that maybe this wouldn't be as hard as I had anticipated. "Well, I think I might like-"

"Oh? So, did you catch the game last night? I was pulling for the Knicks to win."

"Dad, I like...I like-"

"So, pumpkin, have you thought about joining the basketball team this year? I know you like the band, but maybe joining a sport will help you meet more people."

I tried again and again to bring up the topic, but each time my dad would deflect and avoid the conversation. It was as if he was intentionally avoiding the truth, unwilling to confront the reality of my sexuality. And, it wasn't just my sexuality I wanted to discuss. I wanted to tell him about the hitchhiker, but I knew if I couldn't even talk about being a lesbian, I couldn't even try to talk about the latter.

Frustrated and hurt, I eventually gave up trying to talk to him about it. I realized that no matter how much I longed for his understanding and acceptance, it was something I would never receive.

I felt a deep sense of loneliness and isolation, knowing I couldn't confide in the one person who was supposed to always be there for me. I longed to truly have someone to talk to, to share my fears and insecurities with, but unfortunately, I didn't. I just had myself, and the bones in my shed. I reached into my pocket, brushed my fingers across the tiny fragment of bone I kept of her and smiled as I walked back to my room.

And so, I kept my sexuality bottled up inside, hiding a part of myself from the world and from the one person who should have been able to understand me the most. I bottled up every feeling I knew was different and strange from all the other kids at school. It was a heavy burden to carry, one I had no choice but to bear alone.

But, at least I still have her, *I thought,* and maybe I can create more friends.

I stop touching my father's letter and pick up my book. I can't wait much longer to finish *Shadows of Appalachia* by D.L. Winchester, because it is too good to put down. I plan to read until they call chow. Maybe the story will keep my mind away from the memories.

·········

I sit in my cell, trying to focus on the book in my hands. The words blur together as the noise from the other prisoners grows louder and more disruptive. It is impossible to concentrate with the constant shouting, and banging that echo through the cramped space. It is the evening day-room crowd after supper chow, and it is always the loudest because that's when the card tables are set up and sports betters wake up to place bets and sweat numbers.

I close my eyes and take a deep breath, trying to block out the chaos around me. I could care less about who is winning what, or who has the phone line next. All I want to do is read my Bible. Reading the story of Saul, I just want to continue with his journey and learn more about it. I always found solace in reading, an escape from the harsh reality of prison life. But today, even that small comfort is being taken away from me.

I close my eyes and take several deep breaths, calming my nerves and relaxing my mind. Opening my eyes slowly, I am at peace.

I am finally able to dull the noise in my head enough to read. All I have to do is focus on what I am about to read. It is as if God answered my prayer and made it so I can focus on His words.

The only real solace I've found is in reading my Bible. It is my source of comfort, my guiding light in the darkness of my confinement. But just as I am immersing myself in the words of wisdom and hope, a loud knock on the door interrupts my tranquility.

I look up to see a guard standing at the entrance of my cell, his stern expression betraying no hint of sympathy. "You have work duty," he barks, his voice cold and commanding. "Come on. Get up."

Reluctantly, I close my Bible and follow the guard out of my cell. As we walk through the dimly lit corridors of the prison, I can't help but feel a sense of dread creeping over me. Work duty is never a pleasant experience, and I know that whatever task awaits me will be grueling and thankless.

We finally arrive at the prison gym, a stark and barren room filled with the echoes of past sweat, toil, and discarded workout shirts. The guard motions for me to start cleaning, his eyes watching my every move with a critical gaze.

I pick up a mop and bucket, resigning myself to the monotonous task ahead. As I scrub the grimy floors, my mind wanders back to the words of the Bible I had been reading earlier. The verses of forgiveness and redemption seem to mock me in my current predicament, reminding me of the mistakes that led me to this place.

Am I beyond true redemption? Can I be forgiven?

But as I work, a sense of peace begins to wash over me. Despite the harshness of my surroundings, I find solace in the simple act of cleaning. It is a reminder that even in the darkest of times, there is still a glimmer of hope to be found. It is as if I am washing my sins away. I am finally at peace.

"I'm gonna grab a bite. You good?" the guard asks.

"Yeah, sure thing."

"Don't fuck anything up. I'll only be a few minutes."

"You got it. I won't."

· · · · **·** **·** · · · ·

As I clean the bench presses of the prison gym, a voice suddenly pierces through the silence of my quiet work duty. Startled, I turn around to find the same girl who confronted me at the library, standing there, glaring at me with anger and disgust.

"You think you can hide from what you've done, huh?" she spat, her words full of vicious truth. "You're nothing but a worthless piece of trash. You're fucking sick!"

Her words sting me deeply, invoking memories of all my mistakes, and my crimes. Despite my attempts to change and find redemption, her harsh words I know to be true.

Feeling a wave of guilt and shame wash over me, I muster the courage to speak up. "I found God, and I'm trying to make it right," I whisper, hoping she will understand that I am striving to be a better person.

But her face remains cold and unmoved. "Don't give me that pathetic excuse," she scoffs. "You think you can make that shit right? You're fucking sicker than I thought." Her eyes blaze with an intensity that sends shivers down my spine.

Tears well up in my eyes.

And then, she shoves me.

I fall.

I fall hard.

Tripping over the bench press and scraping my arms on the rusty barbell, I find myself in a dangerous situation. As I look up in confusion, I can't help but ask, "What are you doing?"

"It's time you paid for your sins," she says. Her eyes grow wider, and more intense. "God has spoken to me and asked me to carry out His wrath."

I try to crawl away, but she grabs my ankle and pulls me closer to her.

"You can't run from this, bitch!"

In that moment, resignation washes over me, and I brace myself for whatever is to come. "I know," I whisper, accepting my fate.

"Did you take pleasure in their pain? Did you like their suffering?"

"I made sure they were drugged so they wouldn't feel anything," I manage to say as my throat continues to tighten.

"Well," she says as she leans down, taking a barbell in her hand, while never breaking eye contact. "You will feel everything God is going to give you. I am the Lord, and my wrath will strike upon thee!"

I swallow the lump of fear, turning it into a lump of acceptance. I accept this because I know I deserve this, and so much more. It has finally come full circle. The barbell has now exchanged from death-giver to bringing my own end as she swings downward with powerful anger that matches God's wrath.

My last thought before I see nothing is: *even God has left me alone, even God has abandoned me.*

·········

A burst of agony blasts through my entire being, and then my mind wanders. Do you know how it feels to truly feel utterly lonely? I know it all too well. It's an agonizing burden that relentlessly buries itself within the depths of my heart. Every single day, every single hour, I can sense that hole inside me growing, stretching, until there is no shred of possibility left for me to even dare to dream. It's an insatiable void that devours my thoughts, extinguishes my ambitions, and suffocates any glimpse of hope that dares to ignite. Loneliness coils its icy tendrils around me, strangling the very essence of my being, cruelly reminding me of the bleak reality I am condemned to endure.

All I ever yearned for was to be loved, to be cherished. I craved someone who would gaze upon me with such love, believing I was their sole object of affection. Yet, here I am, stranded in solitude, abandoned by love's embrace. My days stretch out like an endless abyss, accompanied solely by the echoes of my own thoughts, which themselves even disdain their dwelling within my mind. No solace can be found in this desolate existence, no warmth to quell the ever-present ache of longing. Each passing moment only serves to remind me of my unfulfilled desires, amplifying the hollowness that seeps into the depths of my weary soul. I have no dreams because my loneliness won't allow them. I only have the compulsion to simply get by each day, because I'm too much of a coward to take my own life.

In the solitude of my existence, lying in the hospital bed, I harbor a quiet longing for recognition, a desperate yearning for connection in the vast emptiness that engulfs me. I cling to the fragile hope, a hope that someday, somewhere, someone may stumble upon my story and think to themselves, "I would've loved her. I would've loved her."

· · · · · · · · · ·

All of a sudden, a flash of white-hot pain, and I see myself when I went to Miami shortly after being discharged from the Army.

It was a much-needed, and much-wanted break from the chaos and stress of military life, and the shame I knew I brought to my dad. The warm sun and salty air were a welcome change from the harsh realities of who I had become.

During my time there, I decided to visit the beach. I hadn't been to the beach before, and the sight of the vast expanse of sand and water brought back memories of simpler times. I found a quiet spot, finished my beer, and began to build a sandcastle, shaping the sand with my hands and creating towers and walls with my fingers.

As I worked on my sandcastle, I couldn't help but think about how fragile it was. One strong wave could easily destroy all my hard work. And yet, there was something beautiful about that. The waves crashing against the shore were both destructive and mesmerizing, much like myself.

Sipping a new beer, my eyes swept over the waves, watching as they slowly crept closer to my sandcastle, knowing that it was only a matter of time before they would wash it away. And when they finally did, I felt a strange sense of peace. It was a reminder that nothing in life is permanent, that beauty can be found in destruction, and that loneliness could finally end.

I got up, drank the last of my beer, opened another one, and started walking back toward the motel I was staying in.

As I walked along the beach, I thought about my time in the Army, right after I flunked out of school, got kicked out of Grandma's, and had to find an apartment of my own. So many things I had seen and done. I had witnessed destruction and chaos, but I had also seen moments of beauty and humanity. I realized that, much like the waves that destroyed my sandcastle, I was both destructive and beautiful all at once.

And then I saw her.

The hitchhiker.

She walked toward me, her footsteps making bloody imprints in the sand. Her clothes were dirty and blood-stained. Her arms were covered in cuts and bruises. But the most horrifying thing was her head. The left side was crushed in, and I could see her brain.

"You did this you know?" she said as a stream of red fell from her lips.

"I know, "my lip quivered and my eyes welled up with tears. "I didn't want to." I finally told the truth out loud, and so I said it again. "I didn't want to."

"I know you didn't," her voice was gentle as another line of crimson ran down her neck from her lips.

"I'm sorry." There was no holding back the tears any longer. "I'm so sorry."

"It's okay," she said, coming closer, and brushing my hair behind my ear. "Really, it's okay."

"No," I said as a snot bubble formed and popped.

"I would've died hooking somewhere, hitching a ride to my inevitable end. My life wasn't going anywhere good."

Her eyes were still that same shade of green that drew me to her in the first place.

"But I didn't...that didn't give me the right to..."

"It's okay. I am at peace, and you should be too."

She kissed me on the cheek, and then just as quickly as she appeared she was gone.

I was just me, even if I were a monster.

I was just me, and at that moment, I was content with myself.

Following in her footsteps, I felt a sense of clarity and acceptance. As I looked out at the endless expanse of the ocean, I knew that I was ready to face whatever lay ahead because I knew I'd never be lonely again, and I never was...

·········

"I think in some way I wanted it to end, even if it meant my own destruction." - Jeff Dahmer

Afterword

I know this story is not historically accurate, and it was never supposed to be. It is a 'what if' type of tale.

Regardless, in writing this book and going into the dark and disturbing mind of Jeff Dahmer, I felt compelled to include this author's note to emphasize the importance of never forgetting the victims of such heinous crimes.

We must remember their names, their lives, and the immense tragedy they endured.

By exploring Jeff's psyche and attempting to understand the complexities behind his actions, we strive to prevent the recurrence of such tragedies in the future.

I hope that this story sheds light on the profound impact of such crimes and contributes to a more compassionate, aware, and vigilant society so that when the warning signs appear, people can seek help.

ACKNOWLEDGEMENTS

I would like to thank my mother for always giving me unwavering support, and encouraging me to pursue my dream of becoming an author. I love you so much, Mama.

D.L Winchester, our friendship is invaluable and priceless. Thank you. Your advice and suggestions played a huge role in helping this story become what it is.

How could I forget Joe Stout? He truly helped this story become what it is now. Without him, it'd still be a small 5,000 words, yet he kept saying, 'I wanna see more!' and kept me writing. And, who can forget Wednesday and Atlas for helping make sure he was balancing life and work in a balance of their own making?

Lastly, thank you, Daniella Dorsch, Asher Dark, Danielle Yvonne, and Paige Ray for reading this project in its early stages and keeping me wanting to write it even when I had doubts about it. Thank you. You're the best.

Special thanks to Wrath James White, Dan Shrader, Jason Nickey, Stuart Bray, Ashley Fox, Chuck Daniels,

Colin Emery, Laura Bilodeau, Nick Scarbrough, Taylor Hull, Crystal Baynam, and Matthew Vaughn.

Thank you to my readers. I couldn't do what I do without any of you.

ABOUT THE AUTHOR

Carietta Dorsch, the self-proclaimed mistress of the spooky, spine-tingling, and downright stomach-churning written art! Since she was a little creature still sleeping in her coffin, she has been utterly enthralled by all things macabre and those hair-raising tales that make you want to sleep with more lights on than the sky has stars.

As a writer, Carietta firmly believes that getting friendly with the dark side can help us uncover significant insights about ourselves and the world around us.

Forget about sunshine and rainbows; let's dive into the wickedly wonderful world of the bloody and gory, both imaginary and real, and discover our humanity's sick and twisted depths.

Strap yourself in as tightly as possible because her goal is always to make this horror-filled ride splatter the walls of your mind!